W9-BZU-833

A Note to Parents

Rhyme, Repetition, and Reading are 3 R's that make learning fun for your child. **Rhyme Time Readers** will introduce your child to the sounds of language, providing the foundation for reading success.

Rhyme

Children learn to listen and to speak before they learn to read. When you read this book, you are helping your child connect spoken language to written language. This increased awareness of sound helps your child with phonics and other important reading skills. While reading this book, encourage your child to identify the rhyming words on each page.

Repetition

Rhyme Time Readers have stories that your child will ask you to read over and over again. The words will become memorable due to frequent readings. To keep it fresh, take turns reading, and encourage your child to chime in on the rhyming words.

Reading

Someday your child will be reading this book to you, as learning sounds leads to reading words and finally to reading stories like this one. I hope this book makes reading together a special experience.

Have fun and take the time to let your child read and rhyme.

Francie Alexander

—Chief Education Officer,
Scholastic's Learning Ventures

To my cousin, Anthony J. Nickols, Jr.,
whose short, but joyous, stay here on
Earth was an example of the greatest
kind of courage in his battle against
Non-Hodgkin's Lymphoma.
Gone too soon and greatly missed,
with love
—A.S.M.

For Ted and Jo
—J.S.

ISBN: 0-439-33403-9

Text copyright © 2001 by Angela Shelf Medearis.
Illustrations copyright © 2001 by Jackie Snider.
All rights reserved. Published by Scholastic Inc.
SCHOLASTIC, RHYME TIME READERS, CARTWHEEL BOOKS,
and associated logos are trademarks and/or registered trademarks of Scholastic Inc.

Library of Congress Cataloging-in-Publication Data available

10 9 8 7 6 5 4 3 2 1   01 02 03 04 05

Printed in the U.S.A.
First printing, November 2001

The Biggest Snowball Fight!

by Angela Shelf Medearis
Illustrated by Jackie Snider

SCHOLASTIC INC.

New York Toronto London Auckland Sydney
Mexico City New Delhi Hong Kong

There's a big clock in our old town.
That clock started
the biggest snowball fight around.

With a *tock* and a *tick*,
and a *tick* and a *tock*,
the hands move slowly
around that big clock.

One night, the snow fell
down, down, down, down.
Snow covered the clock
and every house in town.

The very next day,

little Jimmy McKay

waded through the snow

into town to play.

The clock struck noon

with a loud, booming sound.

That's what started

the biggest snowball fight around.

A huge ball of snow fell
from the face of the clock.
It landed on Jimmy—
oh, what a shock!
Snow slid down Jimmy's coat
and into his pants.
That day he invented
the cold snowball dance.

Jimmy wiggled and jiggled
and danced all around,
until a snowball rolled out
onto the ground.

Sally McGee saw Jimmy

wiggling and jiggling.

He looked so funny —

she couldn't help giggling.

Jimmy saw Sally

having a lot of fun.

Since no one else was around

he thought she was the one.

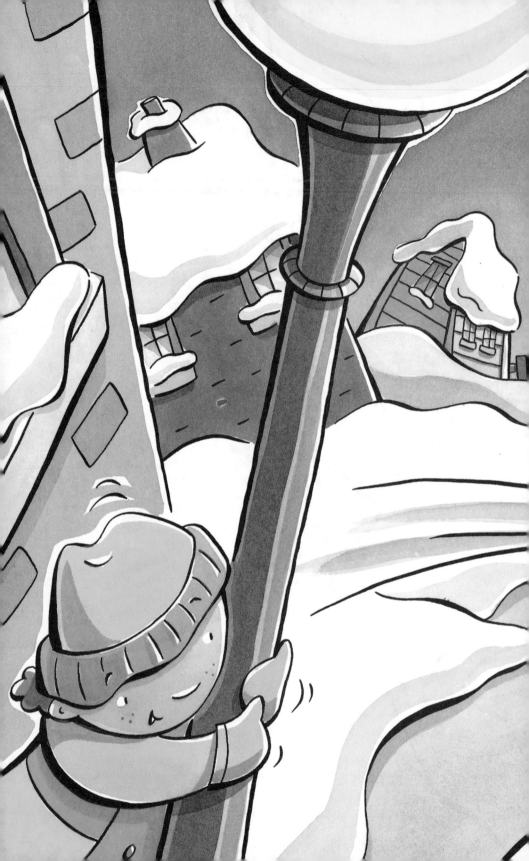

So Jimmy threw a snowball
at Sally McGee.
Then he hid behind a lamppost,
as quick as could be.
The snowball slid down Sally's coat
and into her pants.
That day Sally learned
the cold snowball dance.

Sally wiggled and jiggled
and danced all around,
until the snowball rolled out
onto the ground.

Bill Portermann saw Sally
wiggling and jiggling.
She looked so funny—
he couldn't help giggling.
Sally saw Bill,
and she thought he was the one
who threw the snowball
that ruined her fun.

Sally threw a snowball
at Bill Portermann.
Then she hid
inside her mother's van.
The snowball slid down Bill's coat
and into his pants.
Bill started to do
the cold snowball dance.

Bill wiggled and jiggled
and danced all around,
until the snowball rolled out
onto the ground.

Soon snowballs were flying
from here to there.
Snowballs were flying
everywhere.
Every child in town was doing
the snowball dance.
They were wiggling and jiggling
with snow in their pants.

Finally the mayor was called

to stop the fight.

"Stop throwing snowballs," he said.

"We must do what's right!

No more snowballs

shall be thrown

for the rest of the night!"

Then the clock struck six
with a loud booming sound
and dumped snow on the mayor
and all over the ground.

A snowball slid down his coat
and into his pants.
The mayor started to do
the cold snowball dance.

He wiggled and jiggled
and danced all around.
Then a snowball rolled out
onto the ground.

Well he looked so funny,
everyone started to giggle,
and the whole town
began to wiggle and jiggle.

Now every year,

after the first snowfall,

everyone in town

gathers at town hall.

We all wiggle and jiggle

and dance all around.

Then we have a snowball fight

in the center of town.